The Tale of the Whale

For Pickle Lilly and Scallywag Magoo —K. S.

For Susan and Russell Meek —P.

MARGARET K. McELDERRY BOOKS
An imprint of Simon & Schuster Children's Publishing Division
1230 Avenue of the Americas, New York, New York 10020
Text © 2021 by Karen Swann
Illustration © 2021 by Padmacandra
Book design by Greg Stadnyk © 2022 by Simon & Schuster, Inc.
Originally published in Great Britain in 2021 by Scallywag Press Ltd.

For information about special discounts for bulk purchases, please contact Simon & Schuster Special Sales at 1-866-506-1949 or business@simonandschuster.com.
The Simon & Schuster Speakers Bureau can bring authors to your live event. For more information or to book an event, contact the Simon & Schuster Speakers Bureau at 1-866-248-3049 or visit our website at www.simonspeakers.com.
The text for this book was set in Plantin.
Manufactured in China
1121 SCP
First US Edition
2 4 6 8 10 9 7 5 3 1
Library of Congress Cataloging-in-Publication Data
Names: Swann, Karen, author. | Padmacandra, illustrator.
Title: The tale of the whale / by Karen Swann ; illustrated by Padmacandra.
Description: New York : Margaret K. McElderry Books, an imprint of Simon & Schuster Children's Publishing Division, 2022. | "First published in Great Britain in 2021 by Scallywag Press Ltd." | Audience: Ages 4–8. | Audience: Grades K–1. | Summary: A whale takes a child on adventure across the ocean, and together they explore the wonders of the ocean world, but also the sad state of plastic pollution—and the child returns home to try and help the whale to save his marine home.
Identifiers: LCCN 2021013551 (print) | LCCN 2021013552 (ebook) | ISBN 9781534493940 (hardcover) | ISBN 9781534493957 (ebook)
Subjects: LCSH: Whales—Juvenile fiction. | Plastic marine debris—Juvenile fiction. | Marine pollution—Juvenile fiction. | Environmental protection—Juvenile fiction. | Stories in rhyme. | CYAC: Stories in rhyme. | Whales—Fiction. | Ocean—Fiction. | Plastics—Fiction. | Water—Pollution—Fiction. | Environmental protection—Fiction. | LCGFT: Stories in rhyme.
Classification: LCC PZ8.3.S99346 Tal 2022 (print) | LCC PZ8.3.S99346 (ebook) | DDC [E]—dc23
LC record available at https://lccn.loc.gov/2021013551
LC ebook record available at https://lccn.loc.gov/2021013552

The Tale of the Whale

By Karen Swann

Illustrated by Padmacandra

Margaret K. McElderry Books

New York   London   Toronto   Sydney   New Delhi

Where land becomes sky
and sky becomes sea,
I first saw the whale . . .

and the whale first saw me.

And high on the breeze came his sweet-sounding song—

"I've so much to show you, if you'll come along."

I scrambled aboard in the silvery light

and watched tiny houses drift far out of sight.

We floated away on the rocking-horse sea. . . .

I smiled at the whale
and the whale smiled at me.

We sailed the blue ocean
with turtles and rays,
and tail-splashed the seagulls
in deepwater bays.

We danced with the dolphins that waltzed through the sea. . . .

I laughed with the whale

and the whale laughed with me.

I took a deep breath and we dived through the blue,

and there, on the bottom, a ship with no crew!

But where was the treasure deep under the sea?

I shrugged at the whale and the whale shrugged at me.

We swam over mountains,
through valleys of sand—

an ocean in motion,
a bright, busy land—

with carpets of colors that
breathed with the sea. . . .

I watched with the whale
and the whale watched with me.

We crashed through the surface.
We splashed oh, so high—
a splutter, a rumble, then *whoosh* to the sky!

"I'm flying!" I cried
to the cold, ice-capped sea. . . .

I waved to the whale

and the whale waved to me.

The whale's tummy rumbled, his mouth opened wide,
and half of an ocean was swallowed inside. . . .

I stared at the whale
as he stared back at me—
I understood now
what he'd brought me to see.

A watery trash can of bottles and caps,

some straws, an old toothbrush, and torn plastic wraps;

a net lost while fishing, a large coffee cup—

the soup of the ocean, he'd swallowed it up.

A turtle in trouble,   a gull in distress,

a tightening collar,

a plastic bag mess.

We traveled home saddened
by all we could see. . . .
I cried with the whale
and the whale cried with me.

I gazed in his eyes as I stood on the sand,

and made him a promise to tell the whole land

the tale of the whale and the plastic soup sea.

You've heard the whale's story. . . .

Please, change it with me.